P9-BZT-781

Dear Parents and Educators,

Welcome to Penguin Young Readers! As parents and educators, you know that each child develops at his or her own pace—in terms of speech, critical thinking, and, of course, reading. Penguin Young Readers recognizes this fact. As a result, each Penguin Young Readers book is assigned a traditional easy-to-read level (1–4) as well as a Guided Reading Level (A–P). Both of these systems will help you choose the right book for your child. Please refer to the back of each book for specific leveling information. Penguin Young Readers features esteemed authors and illustrators, stories about favorite characters, fascinating nonfiction, and more!

Young Cam Jansen and the Goldfish Mystery

LEVEL 3

GUIDED READING LEVEL **K**

This book is perfect for a **Transitional Reader** who:
- can read multisyllable and compound words;
- can read words with prefixes and suffixes;
- is able to identify story elements (beginning, middle, end, plot, setting, characters, problem, solution); and
- can understand different points of view.

Here are some **activities** you can do during and after reading this book:
- Compound Words: A compound word is made when two words are joined together to form a new word. *Goldfish* is a compound word that is used in this story. Reread the story and try to find other compound words.
- Chapter Titles: The title of each chapter is very important. It should catch the reader's attention, and should say something about the chapter. Each of the five chapters in this book has a title. Work with the child to come up with a new title for each chapter.

Remember, sharing the love of reading with a child is the best gift you can give!

—Bonnie Bader, EdM
  Penguin Young Readers program

*Penguin Young Readers are leveled by independent reviewers applying the standards developed by Irene Fountas and Gay Su Pinnell in *Matching Books to Readers: Using Leveled Books in Guided Reading*, Heinemann, 1999.

For my grandsons Jacob and Yoni
and for their goldfish Alvin and Simon—DA

To my cousin Matt, who gave his fish a special
home, and to Janet—SN

PENGUIN YOUNG READERS
Published by the Penguin Group
Penguin Group (USA) LLC, 375 Hudson Street, New York, New York 10014, USA

USA | Canada | UK | Ireland | Australia | New Zealand | India | South Africa | China

penguin.com
A Penguin Random House Company

Text copyright © 2013 by David A. Adler. Illustrations copyright © 2013 by Susanna Natti.
All rights reserved. Previously published in hardcover in 2013 by Penguin Young Readers. This edition
published in 2014 by Penguin Young Readers, an imprint of Penguin Group (USA) LLC,
345 Hudson Street, New York, New York 10014. Manufactured in China.

The Library of Congress has cataloged the hardcover edition under
the following Control Number : 2012029603

ISBN 978-0-14-242224-3   10 9 8 7 6 5 4 3 2 1

Young Cam Jansen

and the Goldfish Mystery

by David A. Adler

illustrated by Susanna Natti

Penguin Young Readers
An Imprint of Penguin Group (USA) LLC

Contents

Chapter 1
Test Your Memory

"Ring the bell!

Win a prize!" a woman called.

She was in a large tent at a

charity fair.

Cam Jansen, her friend Eric

Shelton, and Cam's aunt Molly

walked to the tent.

"Try your luck.

Win a teddy bear," the woman said.

"Oh no. I work for an airline,"
Molly told her.

"I'm traveling this afternoon.
These bears are too big
to take on an airplane."

"Test your memory.
Win a prize!"
a man in another tent called out.

Aunt Molly gave the man a dollar.

"Close your eyes, ma'am,"
the man said.

"Is my hair curly or straight?"

"Curly," Aunt Molly answered.

"I'm bald," the man said.

"What color is my shirt?"

"Green."

"It's blue.

You didn't win,"

the man said.

Molly told the man,

"These are Cam and Eric.

They're best friends.

They're always together.

Isn't that nice?"

Molly gave the man two more dollars.

Eric didn't remember that the man

wore eyeglasses.

He didn't win a prize.

Then Cam closed her eyes

and said, "Click!"

"What's my name?" the man asked.

"Your name tag says 'Bill.'

But the letters on your shirt are 'WG.'

So I think Bill is your nickname."

"That's right," Bill said.

"My real name is William."

Cam's eyes were still closed.

"You have a green pen and a blue

pen in your shirt pocket,"

she told Bill.

"You're wearing a watch

with a leather band."

"Okay! Okay!
You win a prize," Bill said.
Eric told Bill, "Cam has a
photographic memory.
It's like she has a camera
and pictures in her head
of everything she's seen.

Her real name is Jennifer,

but we call her Cam.

That's her nickname.

It's short for 'the Camera.'"

Cam told Bill, "*Click!* is the sound

my mental camera makes."

"Here's your prize," Bill said.

He gave Cam a big jar

of red, white, and blue popcorn.

"Wow!" Aunt Molly said.

"I love popcorn!"

Chapter 2
Throw a Ball! Win a Fish!

Cam gave Aunt Molly

the jar of popcorn.

"Thank you," Aunt Molly said.

"Now I'll win something for you."

"Throw a ball and win a fish!"

the man in the Ball Toss tent said.

In the tent was a large table.

On the table were lots of small bowls.

In each bowl was water and a goldfish.

"Throw a ball in a bowl and the
goldfish is yours," the man said.

Lots of people were in the tent.

They were all trying to win goldfish.

"I can do that," Aunt Molly said.

Molly gave the man a dollar.

The man gave her three
Ping-Pong balls.

Molly threw one of the balls.

It hit the edge of a bowl and

bounced off.

Molly threw the other two balls.

They also bounced off the bowls.

Molly gave the man lots of dollars.

She threw lots of Ping-Pong balls.

At last she won two goldfish,

one for Cam and one for Eric.

"I'm naming mine Missy," Cam said.

"I'm naming mine Max," Eric said.

"What should we do next?"

Aunt Molly asked.

"We should go home," Cam told her.

"You have to be at the airport soon."

Cam's father was waiting for them

when they got home.

"You have to hurry," he told Molly.

"We have to get to the airport."

"Please hang up your jackets,"
Cam's mother told Cam and Eric,
"and wash your hands.
Then you can have a snack."

Cam and Eric put their goldfish
on the hall table.
They hung up their jackets
and washed up.

"Good-bye," Molly called to them.
"I have to hurry."

Cam and Eric thanked Molly for
taking them to the fair.
They said good-bye to her.
Then they had a snack
of popcorn and juice.

"We won Missy and Max,"
Eric told Cam's mother.
"They're goldfish."
Cam said, "Aunt Molly
won them for us.
They're in the hall."
"May I see them?" Mrs. Jansen asked.
Cam, Eric, and Mrs. Jansen
went to the hall.
The bowls were there,
but Missy and Max were gone.

Chapter 3
Cam Said, "Click!"

"Are you sure there were fish

in these bowls?"

Mrs. Jansen asked.

"Of course we're sure.

The goldfish were the prizes,"

Eric said.

Cam told her mother,

"No one would want to

win just a bowl of water."

Cam and Eric looked on the table.

They looked on the floor

near the table.

Eric said, "Maybe Missy and Max

swam away."

Cam shook her head.

"Fish need water to swim.

The only water here is in these bowls."

Cam's mom said, "Maybe on the way home the fish jumped out of the bowls."

Cam closed her eyes.

She said, "Click!"

With her eyes still closed she said,

"When we came home

Missy and Max

were still in these bowls.

I can see them in a picture

I have in my head."

Cam said, "Click!" again.

"Now I'm looking at another picture."

She opened her eyes.

She looked at the two bowls and said,

"Missy and Max are not

the only things Aunt Molly

won at the fair that are missing."

Chapter 4
Let's Look for Clues

"Aunt Molly won two bowls

and two goldfish," Eric told Cam.

"That's all she won."

"No," Cam said.

"She also won the water in each bowl.

Each bowl was filled

almost to the top.

Now they are about half filled.

The missing water is a clue.

Let's look for more clues."

They looked in the hall.

"Here's another clue," Cam said.

"There are a few drops of water
on the floor."

Cam and Eric looked in the kitchen
for more clues.

The bowl of popcorn and cups of
juice were still on the table.

Cam said, "That's the red,
white, and blue popcorn
I won at the fair."

Cam opened the cupboards.

"Where's the jar?"

Eric said, "Maybe Aunt Molly
took along the jar with the rest
of the popcorn."

"No," Cam said.

"That jar is too big
to take on an airplane."

Cam's mother came into the kitchen.

"Mom," Cam asked, "did Aunt Molly take any popcorn for her trip?"

"Yes. She put some in that bowl for you. She put the rest in a bag. She put the bag in her jacket pocket. Then she hurried to get to the airport."

"I think she did something else," Cam said.

"I think I solved the goldfish mystery."

Chapter 5
Missy and Max

"Do you remember Bill,
the memory-quiz man?"
Cam asked Eric.
"Do you remember what
Aunt Molly told him?"
"She said he had curly hair
and was wearing a green shirt."
Cam said, "She also told him
we're best friends.

She said we're always together.

She said that was nice."

"It *is* nice," Eric said.

Cam said, "I think she wants

Missy and Max to be together.

I think she cleaned the popcorn jar.

Then she moved Missy and Max

with some of their water into the jar.

That's why there was less water
in the bowls.
That's why there was water on
the floor."
Mrs. Jansen said,
"Molly was in such a hurry.
I bet she forgot to tell us
what she did."
"Hello!" Mr. Jansen called.
"I'm home."
He came into the kitchen.
"I have a strange message from Molly.
Just as she was leaving she said,
'Tell Cam and Eric
the fish are in the sink.'"
"Which sink?" Mrs. Jansen asked.

She looked in the kitchen sink
but didn't find the fish.

"What fish?" Cam's father asked.

Cam told her father
about Missy and Max.

They found the fish in the
popcorn jar.

The jar was in the bathroom sink
next to Molly's room.

Eric said, "She added lots of water.

Missy and Max have

lots of water for swimming."

"We'll take turns," Cam said.

"First the fish will be in my house."

"Then they'll be in my house,"

Eric said.

"But they'll always be together,

just like us."

A Cam Jansen Memory Game

Take another look at the picture on page 6.
Study it.
Blink your eyes and say, "Click!"
Then turn back to this page
and answer these questions:

1. Is Aunt Molly wearing a jacket?
    What color is it?
2. Are Cam and Eric wearing jackets?
3. Are there any dogs in the picture?
4. Is anyone trying the beanbag toss?
5. What color is the one balloon in
    the picture?